Secret of the
SCHOOL SUITOR

By J.L. Anderson
Illustrated by David Ouro

Rourke
Educational Media
rourkeeducationalmedia.com

www.rourkeeducationalmedia.com

Edited by: Keli Sipperley
Cover layout by: Renee Brady
Interior layout by: Jen Thomas
Cover and Interior Illustrations by: David Ouro

Library of Congress PCN Data

Secret of the School Suitor / J.L. Anderson
(Rourke's Mystery Chapter Books)
ISBN (hard cover)(alk. paper) 978-1-63430-383-5
ISBN (soft cover) 978-1-63430-483-2
ISBN (e-Book) 978-1-63430-578-5
Library of Congress Control Number: 2015933739

Printed in the United States of America, North Mankato, Minnesota

Dear Parents and Teachers:

With twists and turns and red herrings, readers will enjoy the challenge of Rourke's Mystery Chapter Books. This series set at Watson Elementary School builds a cast of characters that readers quickly feel connected to. Embedded in each mystery are experiences that readers encounter at home or school. Topics of friendship, family, and growing up are featured within each book.

Mysteries open many doors for young readers and turn them into lifelong readers because they can't wait to find out what happens next. Readers build comprehension strategies by searching out clues through close reading in order to solve the mystery.

This genre spreads across many areas of study including history, science, and math. Exploring these topics through mysteries is a great way to engage readers in another area of interest. Reading mysteries relies on looking for patterns and decoding clues that help in learning math skills.

Whether readers are reading the books independently or you are reading with them, engaging with them after they have read the book is still important. We've included several activities at the end of each book to make this both fun and educational.

Do you think you and your reader have what it takes to be a detective? Can you solve the mystery? Will you accept the challenge?

Rourke Educational Media

Table of Contents

The Bus Mishap

The fog was thick enough that Divya's socks felt damp and itchy against her ankle braces. She bent down to adjust her socks underneath the braces and watched as a whirl of orange-ish-yellow zoomed right past her. Oh no—that was her school bus! How could Bus Driver McCool miss picking her up?

"Wait!" Divya called and chased after Bus 72. Running wasn't easy with her weak ankle joints but walking to school all the way down North Drew Lane and then across Centerville Highway to get to Watson Elementary School was next to impossible. Just as Divya started to plan what she would do instead of going to school, Bus 72 slammed to a stop.

Bus Driver McCool extended the stop sign and then swerved the oversized school bus in reverse. Divya thought he was going to bump into the curb, but he stopped in time.

"Sorry!" he said as he cranked the doors open. He lowered his voice as he asked Divya, "You're not going to tell Mrs. Holmes or Mr. Sleuth about this little mishap, are you?"

Divya had been too shocked about Bus Driver McCool almost forgetting to pick her up and then driving so crazy that she hadn't thought about telling Mrs. Holmes, the principal, or Mr. Sleuth, the school secretary.

"I really am sorry," Bus Driver McCool said. He sure did look upset the way his thick eyebrows frowned along with his whole thin face. In fact, the bus driver looked tired, and he reminded Divya of the way her father came home exhausted when he used to work at the hospital. Her dad still looked that way sometimes when he had to work overnight shifts at Centerville Nursing Home. Divya's dad often took care of Bus Driver McCool's mother there.

This was the first time any sort of mishap of any kind had happened. Divya liked that Bus Driver McCool picked her up at a special stop over a block and a half from the real bus stop so she didn't have to walk so far. He was always nice to everyone, even Klaude, who could be super annoying. Plus, Bus Driver McCool cranked out the best music on the radio. He knew how to carry a tune when he sang along with the songs.

"It's okay," Divya said. She was about to make her way down the bus aisle to sit next to her friend Javier, but she spied a small piece of paper near her foot.

Divya picked up the paper and almost threw it in the garbage bin near the driver's seat, then she saw it was a receipt.

A florist receipt with the name Fenton McCool on it to be exact, she noticed. Divya handed it to the bus driver.

"Oh, thanks," Bus Driver McCool said, shoving the receipt into the pocket of his faded jeans that had large rips in the knees. *Did he just turn red?* Divya thought to herself.

Javier's sketchbook sat on his lap when Divya took her spot next to him—only he wasn't drawing dragons or space cats like he usually does. He stretched his neck from side to side

and gave it a quick rub.

"You okay?" Divya asked.

"I never knew a bus could stop that fast," Javier said. "I heard Bus Driver McCool used to be a race car driver but I never believed it until now."

"I heard he ran over some kid's bike at his old driving job and then got fired," Klaude said.

Divya shot Klaude her most stern look for listening in on her private conversation with Javier. It was nowhere near as stern as the look

Mrs. Holmes gave to the students at Watson Elementary when they were out of line, but Divya was practicing. The look must've worked because Klaude went back to fiddling with what looked like a wooden musical instrument.

"Well I heard Bus Driver McCool applied for a job as a security officer where my mom works," a girl named Queeneka whispered to her group of friends. "He could use some extra money to buy himself some nicer clothes. That's the second time he wore that bright green shirt this week." Queeneka was really into fashion.

Divya hadn't noticed the green shirt before.

Was Bus Driver McCool looking for a new job, or was he going to work a second job?

As Bus Driver McCool drove the remaining route to school, Javier drew a silly looking cat peeking out of a rocket ship. Divya got lost in thought about the receipt and how strange Bus Driver McCool was acting. Then something even stranger happened.

Divya Decides to Help

"Hold on tight!" Bus Driver McCool cried out. He revved the bus engine. Divya looked up just in time to see that the bus driver nearly ran a red light. Some small car honked as the school bus roared by. Maybe their bus driver really had been a race car driver!

"I'm calling my lawyer," Klaude said once Bus Driver McCool slowed down. Several kids on the bus laughed.

Leave it to Klaude to make a joke. Divya didn't want to think about Bus Driver McCool getting in serious trouble. All year long and all last year, Bus Diver McCool had been the best bus driver ever. Something was up. Divya was determined to figure it out.

"See you in a few minutes," Divya said to

Javier. She took her time getting off the bus so she would have a chance to talk to Bus Driver McCool without nosy people like Klaude listening in.

Divya was surprised to see a black suit hanging behind the bus driver's seat. She hadn't noticed it when she boarded the bus, but then again, she was too caught off guard. Not to mention finding the bizarre receipt. Queeneka hadn't noticed the suit either or else she wouldn't have made that comment about his clothes.

Bus Driver McCool wasn't the type to get dressed up. The fanciest thing Divya ever saw Bus Driver McCool wear was a button down shirt when he attended Back to School Night with Coach Shorts. Though there were lots of rumors about the bus driver, everyone at Watson knew for a fact that Bus Driver McCool was crazy about Coach Shorts.

Just as Bus Driver McCool started to apologize to Divya again, she cut him off. "Is everything okay?"

His shoulders sagged. "I, well, I have big plans and there is a lot going on right now."

Like that could count as a real explanation! Divya waited for him to say more but then he added, "Thanks for your concern but I shouldn't say anything to anyone else. Things are complicated enough. I need to take care of a few things on campus so you'll have to excuse me."

Divya must have looked upset because Bus Driver McCool smiled at her as he helped her down the bus stairs. "Thanks for being such a nice kid."

"Thanks for being such a nice bus driver," she said.

Bus Driver McCool laughed. "I'm not a perfect one, that's for sure!"

Bus Driver McCool left the bus parked in the front of the school with the flashers on. Divya didn't know much about driving a bus, but she did know that the bus probably should've been parked in a different spot.

Javier stood waiting for Divya near the sidewalk, ready to walk to morning assembly together. "What's going on?" he asked.

"Something's up with Bus Driver McCool," she said.

"No joke," Javier said. "Maybe his mom's sick and he's worried about her."

Why hadn't Divya thought of that sooner? Her dad hadn't said anything about Mrs. McCool getting sick, but maybe the flowers were for her. Then another thought worried her. Maybe Bus Driver McCool found out that his mom didn't have much longer to live and the suit was going to be for her funeral!

Divya watched as Bus Driver McCool walked away. She was curious about the things he needed to take care of. "I want to help him," she said.

"I know, but how?" Javier asked.

The other students had gone into the school, and morning assembly would start in a few minutes. "I'm going to follow him to see what I can find out. The more we know, the more we can help," she said.

"You could get into some serious trouble," Javier said.

Divya shrugged. "I almost missed a day of school this morning. I'm not too worried." Other than staying home sick a few days when she came down with the flu, she hadn't missed much school. Besides, teachers didn't take attendance until after morning assembly. If she made it to class before then, she'd never get into any trouble.

Divya should've reported to the cafeteria with Javier, but she tiptoed – or at least tried to tiptoe the best her ankles would allow – after Bus Driver McCool. He walked so fast that she could barely see him in the distance. Good thing he wore that grubby old lime green shirt so it was easy to keep track of him.

"Don't get caught, Divya," Javier called out as he walked in the opposite direction.

"Shh! I don't plan to," she said. "But don't jinx me."

Busted!

Bus Driver McCool climbed up the stairs swiftly. Divya had a hard time keeping up with him, but she kept an eye on that shirt.

She suspected he was going to spend some time with Coach Shorts since they seemed to like to spend so much time together. Divya once saw them eating at the Burger Trough when she ate there with her dad not that long ago. Talk about weird! To see her bus driver and her coach together outside of school. They were even holding hands!

Instead of walking down the long hallway to the gymnasium, Bus Driver McCool took a left to the brightly lit main office. What kind of business did the bus driver need to take care of in the school office?

Divya dipped down low by a red brick wall

near the open door.

"I'm not sure if you saw the 'no parking' sign or not," Mr. Sleuth said. "And in case you didn't know, the sign means 'no parking.'" The school secretary laughed at his own joke.

From what Divya could see by the wall, Bus Driver McCool didn't find the comment funny. "I don't plan on staying here for very long. That's what the flashers flashing on the bus means, in case you didn't know."

He said something else but Divya couldn't hear. Mr. Sleuth folded his gangly arms across his chest. "You have a bone to eat? You parked in a no parking zone to tell me that?"

Bus Driver McCool spoke up much louder. "No! Not a bone to eat. I have a bone to pick with you!"

The two of them went back and forth. Divya really wished she could hear what they were saying. She could only make out bits of the conversation, something about Mr. Sleuth was making things extra challenging.

Divya inched forward to get a better listen, but then she stumbled and caught herself against

the glass window of the office.

Mr. Sleuth walked over to see what had happened.

Busted!

Divya had to think of an excuse for being there. Fast!

"Is there something I can help you with, Divya, or are you just testing gravity in the office?" Mr. Sleuth asked.

Divya laughed like his joke was a lot funnier than it actually was and then she tried to think of something clever to say in return. "Duck! I thought I saw a duck coming for me," she said.

Mr. Sleuth chuckled. "I'll have to remember that."

Bus Driver McCool looked at Divya with his eyebrows squished together in concern. He probably thought she had come to rat on him for his bad driving this morning! She wanted to explain that she was just here to help him, but she had to keep her mission to herself. That was the point of spying, after all.

Divya needed to think quickly.

"I'm here to see the nurse to get a bandage.

I'm getting a blister," she said, pointing at her ankle brace. Maybe Bus Driver McCool would remember the way she was fixing her sock when he nearly missed picking her up earlier. He'd think that she was telling the truth rather than trying to get him in trouble.

Truth be told, a bandage would help keep the skin on her foot from getting more irritated.

Mr. Sleuth pointed her in the direction of Nurse Strongman's office as if she didn't know where to go.

Nurse Strongman had a bandage waiting for her the moment Divya stepped into her office. She was obviously listening in to the office happenings just like her.

"What are those two talking about?" Divya dared to ask. She didn't want to seem too interested in the situation or else Nurse Strongman would catch on that she was faking the blister.

"Adult stuff," Nurse Strongman said, as if it made all the sense in the world.

Ugh. She wasn't any closer to finding out answers.

Divya was just going to take the bandage and leave, but she decided to put it on now in case she could overhear the rest of the conversation between Bus Driver McCool and Mr. Sleuth from the nurse's office.

"Please don't ruin things," she thought she overheard Bus Driver McCool say.

"I'll try. I know you have lots of things to worry about, but your priority needs to be on keeping the students safe. I heard through the grapevine that you gave the students an interesting ride this morning," Mr. Sleuth said.

How in the world did he have time to hear that? Mr. Sleuth seemed to know everything happening at the school all the time, but this seemed unusually fast. Klaude had a big mouth and Divya figured he'd been blabbing.

Hopefully Bus Driver McCool wouldn't blame Divya for word spreading around.

"You're going to miss the rest of morning assembly, young lady," Nurse Strongman said, snapping Divya out of the moment.

Before she left, Divya petted the stuffed school mascot that sat on Nurse Strongman's desk for good luck. It was a while owl with a pair of thick rimmed glasses that looked like it had an important case to solve.

Divya's case certainly felt important and she needed all the good luck she could get.

Chapter four

The Sneaky Spy

Divya stepped up quickly as Bus Driver McCool left the office. "Thanks," she said to Nurse Strongman and then thanked Mr. Sleuth. She made sure to limp even more so they would believe her about the blister. It didn't take too much work thanks to all the running around she'd done this morning.

When Divya left the office, she didn't see the bright green shirt anywhere. Had Bus Driver McCool gone to move the bus and take it to wherever buses went after dropping off the kids? She backtracked on the campus, the same way she walked after getting off the bus.

The custodian was cleaning something out in the front courtyard and waved at her. Divya waved back and tried not to look guilty. She pretended she lost a hair clip and then gave up once the custodian moved on.

Divya didn't see a trace of Bus Driver McCool. The bus was still parked in the no parking zone, the flashers still flashing.

Mr. Sleuth wouldn't be too happy about that. She hoped he wasn't going to move the bus or call the cops to come give the bus driver a ticket. If the rumor about the bus driver running over a kid's bike was true, maybe a ticket would be enough to get him fired.

New rumors about the bus driver from this morning's mishap were already starting to spread, thanks to Klaude, Queeneka, or really, whoever was on the bus.

Divya decided to follow a hunch as to where she thought Bus Driver McCool might have gone. To see Coach Shorts, of course! If he wasn't there, well then she had to give up her mission and get on with her school day.

She picked up her pace once again, happy she had the bandage on her foot. Up the hallway ahead, Divya spied something bright. Something lime green.

Yes! She'd caught up to Bus Driver McCool.

No! He turned around to see who was following him in the hallway. She'd made too much noise.

Divya ducked down behind a three-dimensional bulletin board of a tree with branches growing along the wall. It was supposed to be a story tree. Javier helped build the branches by twisting up a bunch of butcher block paper and taping it together.

Bus Driver McCool scratched his almost bald head and walked on toward the gymnasium.

Whew—that was close.

Divya couldn't wait to tell Javier how his artwork had saved her from almost getting caught yet again.

Things were getting more risky, especially since morning assembly would be over soon. Teachers and students were about to flood the hallways. Her teacher, Mr. Smartline, would soon wonder where she was and would mark her absent. Then he'd call her dad at home, probably waking him up in a bad mood after finally getting to sleep.

Divya hugged the hallway as she crept forward and stood close to the doorframe.

Coach Shorts—who was actually tall and always wore gym pants, not shorts –gave Bus Driver McCool a big hug. She was several inches taller than the bus driver.

"What a surprise to see you!" Coach Shorts said to him. "I didn't expect to see you until later."

"I can't wait for our dinner tonight," Bus Driver McCool said.

"About that," Coach Shorts said, "Can I get a

rain check? The basketball game got rescheduled and I have to be there to coach my team."

Bus Driver McCool said something in a low voice—too low for Divya to hear but she could sense his sadness all over again. He sure seemed to be having a rough day. Divya wondered what she could do to change things.

"I can't reschedule," Coach Shorts responded. "I have to be there. If you love me, then you'll understand."

"Of course I love you and of course I understand," Bus Driver McCool said.

Klaude would've made gagging noises if he'd heard this, Divya thought.

Coach Shorts gave Bus Driver McCool another hug before he left. Coach Shorts may or may not have noticed, but Divya could see that his shoulders sagged even more.

Poor guy.

Poor guy who was walking straight toward Divya!

Chapter five

McCool's Mystery Solved?

As Bus Driver McCool approached her, Divya leaned forward and picked up an empty desk. She pretended she was the custodian and walked the desk inside the classroom. She put on such a good performance in that moment that she decided to try out for the school play later that spring.

Bus Driver McCool passed her by, not noticing who she was or what she was doing. He muttered to himself, "I give up."

"I give up?" Those were dangerous words. Divya couldn't let him give up.

Mr. Hambrick, one of the other third grade teachers, gave Divya a funny look as she stood in the doorframe carrying the empty desk. "Oops!

Wrong room," Divya said with confidence.

She stepped out of the room and set it back in the hallway. Klaude raised an eyebrow at her as he passed her by and so did Queeneka.

Yikes! Morning assembly was over—Divya had to hurry and she was no closer to cracking the case!

Up ahead, she saw the principal, Mrs. Holmes step out of the cafeteria wearing a pair of jeans in much better shape than the bus driver's and a black shirt with the school owl mascot standing on top of a basketball. She seemed even more eager for the basketball game tonight than Coach Shorts.

Bus Driver McCool caught up with Mrs. Holmes. Was he turning himself in for his bad driving?

Divya wished more than anything that she could hear what they were talking about. She'd tried to learn how to read lips to be a better detective, but whenever she tried before, it just looked like the person said watermelon over and over again.

She stopped to really focus on Bus Driver

McCool's face. "Can we talk?" he seemed to ask to Mrs. Holmes.

That had to be it! Mrs. Holmes nodded her head and the two of them walked off in the direction of the office.

Someone bumped into Divya. She yelped in surprise.

"Whoa," Javier said, "I didn't mean to scare you. What did you find out?"

Divya put a finger over her lips to keep him from saying anything else where the entire third grade could hear. She walked over to the bulletin board story tree so they could hide in the hallway.

The first thing Divya told him about was how his artwork saved the day. Javier smiled so wide she could see all of his teeth. Javier had really nice teeth.

Divya told Javier about the flower receipt and the suit. "I wish I could call my dad to find out if his mom is sick or not."

"Now that I've been thinking about it, he probably would've told you about his mom when you asked him how things are going,"

Javier said. "Your dad knows his mom and it's not something he would keep a secret, right?"

"Right." Time was ticking by way too fast. Mr. Smartline would be taking attendance any minute now.

Divya and Javier talked even faster about the rumors and about the conversation that Divya overheard between Bus Driver McCool and Mr. Sleuth.

Was Bus Driver McCool planning on working as a security officer? Had he gotten in trouble at his old job and the crimes were catching up to him?

Things didn't seem to be going too well with Coach Shorts according to Divya—the coach chose the basketball game over their date.

When Divya shared how Bus Driver McCool said he was giving up, everything started to click into place.

The suit, which is something he might wear to a job interview.

The tension with Mr. Sleuth.

The bad driving.

The way the bus driver seemed stressed out.

These things reminded Divya of the way her dad acted right before he quit his nursing job at the hospital to take the nursing home job where he was now much happier. Divya shared her hypothesis.

"Maybe," Javier said. "What about the flower receipt?"

Well, the flowers seemed out of place, they both agreed. Perhaps the flowers weren't related to the case at all.

"I have to stop Bus Driver McCool from quitting Watson Elementary School!"

The bell rang right at that moment. "Cover for me," Divya said.

"Not again," Javier said. He mumbled something else but Divya didn't have time to listen.

Divya to the Rescue

"Did you miss me that much?" Mr. Sleuth said as Divya rushed into the office. He placed his hand over his heart and gave her a cheesy smile.

Divya wanted to think of a funny reply, but she was too focused on saving Bus Driver McCool's job.

All Divya could think of to explain her return was point to Nurse Strongman's office. She hoped Mr. Sleuth would get the hint that she needed yet another bandage. It worked because he nodded and she took off.

Only Divya didn't walk into the nurse's office, she barged right into Mrs. Holmes' office. She wasn't sure who looked more shocked to see

her—the principal or the bus driver.

Even though she was a small woman and wore the basketball shirt featuring the cute owl, Mrs. Holmes looked tough. She reminded Divya of the grandma judge on the TV show who sent criminals to jail.

"I can tell you have something urgent to say to me, but now isn't a good time. As you can see, I'm in a meeting with Mr. McCool," Mrs. Holmes said. "Why don't you set up an appointment with Mr. Sleuth if you would like to talk with me?" Mrs. Holmes asked, though it seemed more like a demand to Divya.

"It can't wait!" Divya said.

Bus Driver McCool turned to Mrs. Holmes. "I can explain why she's here."

Wait, what? Divya thought. How could he possibly know she was here to try to save him from quitting his job? Was she that bad of a spy? Who might've overheard her talking to Javier in the hallway? Divya thought she'd been a pretty decent detective up until now.

"You see, I was distracted and didn't perform my best driving skills. And I, well, might've implied that Divya should keep her concerns to herself which is irresponsible of me," Bus Driver McCool said.

"No, no, no! That's not why I'm here at all!" Divya said, though it came out much more like a shout because she was so worked up about things. She hadn't barged into their meeting to force a confession like this out of him.

"What are you doing, then?" Bus Driver McCool sat up a little straighter and scratched his balding head again.

Mrs. Holmes narrowed her eyes. "Why don't you take a seat?" she said in that calm way of hers. It was another question, but once again, it felt like a demand.

After Divya sat down, she fidgeted with her ankle braces and then tried to explain why she was really here. This was her moment to save Bus Driver McCool's job and she wasn't doing so well so far.

"This morning's ... mishap wasn't a big deal at all. It was foggy and we all got to school safe and sound. That's the important part," Divya said, trying to sound as calm as Mrs. Holmes.

"I'm here because I don't want you to quit driving the school bus. I'm sure that I can speak for all of the students here at Watson to say how much we need you to keep driving Bus 72," she said.

Bus Driver McCool smiled at Divya. "You think I'm quitting?"

Divya could hear the laughter in his voice. Even Mrs. Holmes tried to hide her smile.

Uh oh. Divya had been sure that all clues pointed to the bus driver quitting. "Is everything okay with your mom?" she asked. Since he didn't seem to be leaving his job, maybe the suspicion about his mom's illness had been correct.

"My mom's great, other than stealing some of the snacks from the nursing home kitchen. Thanks for asking. I'm curious why you think I'm quitting," Bus Driver McCool said.

Divya shared her evidence, starting with the rumors. Big mistake.

Mrs. Holmes shook her head. "Rumors should never be at the center of solving a case."

"True, but I have evidence," Divya said. She stopped talking for a moment because she'd started to doubt whether she had solid evidence or not. "At least I thought I did."

If she shared what evidence she had, Divya would have to admit she'd been spying on the bus driver and that she'd skipped morning assembly. She wanted to help the bus driver, but she could be hurting herself.

"We're waiting," Mrs. Holmes said.

Divya needed to choose her words carefully.

Mystery Solved For Real?

Divya explained how she found the receipt and saw the suit. "When I went to get a bandage, I heard you and Mr. Sleuth arguing," she said, looking at Bus Driver McCool.

"Then I heard you say you give up after you talked to Coach Shorts," Divya said. At least the bandage sounded like a valid reason for being in the office, but she couldn't come up with a reason for why she'd followed Bus Driver McCool all the way to the gymnasium. Fortunately, neither one of them asked for her reason.

"I can see why you thought I was quitting," Bus Driver McCool said. That made Divya feel somewhat better that he at least understood.

"I applaud your detective work and your

concern for our staff," Mrs. Holmes said. "Everyone here at Watson Elementary cares very much about Mr. McCool. He is not planning on quitting nor am I going to fire him." Mrs. Holmes brushed her thick bangs to the side of her forehead. She still had a hint of a smile on her face.

This was wonderful news, but there were still a whole lot of unanswered questions. "What was the argument about with Mr. Sleuth, then?" Divya asked.

"That's between the two of them," Mrs. Holmes said.

This was yet another one of those adult responses that Divya found super unhelpful.

Now Divya was the one with her shoulders sagging. She'd gone through all of this trouble and it didn't seem like she'd ever get an answer.

Divya's day started with Bus Driver McCool apologizing to her and now she was apologizing to him and to Mrs. Holmes. "I'm sorry for snooping and missing morning assembly. I wanted to help but it turns out I've made a mess of things."

Divya waited for Mrs. Holmes to explain how much trouble she was in. She dreaded having to call her dad to tell him that she'd been up to no good even if her heart had been in the right place.

"I've always thought you're a nice kid," Bus Driver McCool repeated. It sure was nice to hear after Divya was feeling low.

"I shouldn't say anything, but you've gone through all this trouble for me," he said, and looked over at Mrs. Holmes who shrugged her shoulders.

"You're free to talk to whoever you want to, but you've already seen the consequences of loose lips," the principal said.

What in the world did that mean? Divya's brain was running out of clues.

"You see, I have been working an extra job in the evenings so I could buy something nice for Coach Shorts. Something expensive. As you know, I care about her very much. When I was shopping, I ran into Mr. Sleuth," he said.

"I was so excited that I told him about my plan without thinking about it. Mr. Sleuth has been dropping hints to a few people, and worse, he's been teasing Coach Shorts how she better be prepared to get a special gift from me," Bus Driver McCool said. "That's why I had a bone to pick with him."

Loose lips. Now it made sense. Mr. Sleuth could sometimes be a busybody and he wasn't nearly as good as Divya at keeping a secret.

Divya ran through all the clues again. So the rumor about the second job had been true. No wonder Bus Driver McCool seemed more tired than usual.

She thought about the suit.

The receipt for flowers.

The special, expensive gift.

"You're going to propose to Coach Shorts!" Divya just about shouted, but lowered her voice since other workers in the office might hear her and the secret was already getting out, thanks to Mr. Sleuth.

"Yes," Bus Driver McCool said. "Today is our anniversary and I planned on asking her to marry me at dinner tonight. Only problem is—"

"She cancelled dinner tonight because of the

basketball game," Divya said.

"Try as I might," Mrs. Holmes said, "but I can't reschedule the game. I appreciate you coming by to share the news with me, Mr. McCool, and I'm sorry I can't do more to help you."

"I know how to help you!" Divya said, this time much more sure of herself.

Chapter eight

Divya Saves the Day

Much to her surprise, both Bus Driver McCool and Mrs. Holmes liked her idea. Before Divya went back to class, Mrs. Holmes lectured her about respecting privacy and the importance of attending every part of school, even if an interesting case came up.

Mrs. Holmes gave her a hall pass so she wouldn't get in trouble with Mr. Smartline for being late. "I expect you to explain things to your dad without me having to call him," she said.

"That's more than fair," Divya said. When she walked out of Mrs. Holmes' office, Nurse Strongman stood in the doorway to see what was going on. Mr. Sleuth stood up at his desk, his eyes wide with curiosity.

"Divya, what was going on in there?" Mr. Sleuth asked. "I thought you were on your way to get a bandage."

Like Divya was going to say anything! She needed to recruit some help and she'd fill her friends in on an as-needed basis. Hopefully even Klaude would help.

"I have to get to class," she said. "Thanks for your help today, Mr. Sleuth!"

"So glad you could finally join us," Mr. Smartline said as Divya passed him the note from Mrs. Holmes. "Are you finished helping the orphans?"

Was that code for something? Regardless, she was done lying and sneaking around. "Sorry, I had a case to solve."

Mr. Smartline shook his head. "Very well. Please take a seat, Divya, and pass in your homework."

Javier leaned over to whisper to Divya a few minutes later when their teacher was distracted at the computer. "Sorry," he said. "I came up with a lousy cover story for you. Tell me what happened!"

Orphans! Divya had to keep herself from laughing. "Let's talk at recess. Round up everyone you know," she whispered.

The morning had been stressful and things didn't get any easier as Divya had to wait until recess time.

Javier promised to put his art skills to good use.

"I'll help," Queeneka said after Divya swore everyone to secrecy and shared her plan.

Queeneka loved to be the star at everything, so this wasn't a surprise to Divya. All of Queeneka's friends agreed to help, too.

Soon, everyone else was in on the plan, too. Except Klaude. He just had to complicate things.

"What's in it for me?" Klaude asked.

"To be nice and to help someone who looks after us?" Divya said.

Klaude rubbed his neck like Javier had earlier in the day. "I'll think about it," he said.

Grrrr!

If Klaude wasn't going to help, he would hopefully keep his mouth shut. The team already had their hands full to keep Mr. Sleuth busy and

to prevent him from ruining the surprise for Coach Shorts.

******

Divya dressed up for the basketball game in her Watson Elementary School shirt with the owl mascot on it and the fanciest thing she owned, a jean skirt. She slapped a couple of owl stickers on her ankle braces to show school spirit.

Her dad wore a matching shirt and a pair of dress slacks. She told her dad everything so Mrs. Holmes wouldn't have to. He gave her a similar lecture, but added, "I'm proud of you for caring about others."

Divya wasn't the one about to propose, but her hands felt damp, much damper than her socks had felt this morning. Javier passed out cards for those in on the plan to hold in the air at the right time.

Divya could hardly sit still in the bleachers and to make matters worse, the Owls were losing.

Coach Shorts gave the basketball players a pep talk during the break. Right after the group

high-fived, Mr. Sleuth started to walk right up to Coach Shorts.

What horrible timing! Bus Driver McCool had just waltzed into the gymnasium wearing his black suit and was carrying a rose bouquet so huge Divya could hardly see his face.

Just then, Klaude stood up and played a song on his wooden musical instrument he'd been messing with on the bus. Coach Shorts turned away from Mr. Sleuth and looked out into the bleachers to see where the noise was coming from. Divya could hardly believe Klaude had come to the rescue!

At that moment, Divya and the others held up the signs Javier painted: **"McCool has a ?"**

Bus Driver McCool dropped down to one knee in front of Coach Shorts and asked her to marry him. The crowd went wild when Coach Shorts said yes. Mrs. Holmes wiped a tear from her eye.

What an exciting case—Divya couldn't wait for the bus ride tomorrow so she and the others could recap one of the best proposals in all of Centerville!

How to Solve a Mystery

To solve a mystery, you have to pay attention to the details. When Bus Driver McCool was acting strangely, I tried to find some clues as to why. Well, the flower receipt clue actually found me.

The black suit was another clue. At first it seemed like Bus Driver McCool might be wearing it to his mom's funeral. That was a really sad thought.

There were lots of rumors about the bus driver, but a good detective has to sort fact from fiction. To figure out what is really going on, you have to do some investigating. I snooped around and listened to Bus Driver McCool talk to Mr. Sleuth and then to Coach Shorts. When the bus driver got upset and asked to speak with the principal, Mrs. Holmes, it seemed like Bus Driver McCool was going to quit his job.

I couldn't let that happen! When I tried to save his job, I realized I'd misread some of the clues. Bus Driver McCool wasn't quitting his job at Watson Elementary School. He had taken on a second job to buy something special for Coach Shorts. Then the flowers and the suit made sense!

A Different Point of View
Q & A with Javier
What did you think was going on with Bus Driver McCool?
I knew something was up but at first I didn't have a clue. I thought maybe it was because he was worried about his mom. When my mom got sick, I worried about her a lot and had a hard time focusing at school. I also thought he'd been a race car driver before he became a bus driver. That's still a mystery I want to figure out!

How did you help Divya get to the bottom of the mystery?
I didn't do all the snooping that Divya did,

56

but I covered for her a couple of times.
Mr. Smartline asked me where Divya was
at morning assembly.

"She's helping someone," I said. What else
was I supposed to say? Mr. Smartline
didn't ask me any other questions and I
was really happy about that. Then Divya
asked me to cover for her again when
she missed class.

"Where is Divya now?" Mr. Smartline asked
me.

"She's uh, helping, uh..."

"Orphans," Klaude whispered. He's always
joking.

For some reason, I repeated him. "She's
helping orphans."

Mr. Smartline laughed. My answer didn't
really solve the mystery but it helped buy
Divya some time.

What would you have done differently?
I think I would've joined Divya on her
search for answers instead of waiting

around for her. That made me too nervous! Spying on people would've been more fun but we probably would've gotten caught much easier.

What was your favorite part about the case?
I had a lot of fun making the signs for the students to hold up to get Coach Shorts' attention. I even used pink paint to make it look extra nice. That's my least favorite color.

How do you plan on asking someone to marry you someday?
Ick! I don't think I want to get married. But if I have to, I'll think holding up signs is a good idea. I might do that, only at a football game.

Discussion Questions

1. What did you suspect Bus Driver McCool was up to?
2. Which character did you identify most with, and why?
3. Why do you think Klaude played the musical instrument the night of the basketball game?
4. If you had to rewrite the book from a different character's point of view, who would you pick, and why?
5. List two red-herrings (false clues) that could be added to throw Divya off.
6. How else could Bus Driver McCool have asked Coach Shorts to marry him?

Vocabulary

Here is a list of some important words in the story. Try to use the words in a sentence. You can play a game of memory with the vocabulary words. Write each word on a separate card. Then write the definition on a different set of cards. Mix up the cards and place them face down on a flat surface. With a partner, take turns flipping over two cards each. If the cards make a pair, you get another turn. The person with the most sets of cards at the end of the game wins.

backtrack: trace your steps again
confession: admit the truth
evidence: proof
flashers: lights that flash on a vehicle
hypothesis: theory, educated guess
lectured: taught, scolded
mishap: an accident or mistake
receipt: a proof of payment

revved: increased power

suspected: believed

suspicion: a feeling or thought

three-dimensional: solid, has length, width, and depth

Writing Prompt

1. Using one of the characters from the story as your main character, write a mystery about a bus driver who goes missing. What happened to the bus driver? Who finds the bus driver and how?
2. Write a mystery about a stolen ring. How does your main character find the ring, discover who took it, and get the ring back to the right owner?
3. Describe a crime that uses these vocabulary words: confession, evidence, backtracked, and revved. How does the crime get solved?

Websites to Visit

Divya's weak ankles are caused by cerebral palsy. Here is a link you can visit to learn more:
http://kidshealth.org/kid/health_problems/
   brain/cerebral_palsy.html

Here is a link to learn more about bus safety:
http://www.nhtsa.gov/people/injury/buses/
   kidsschoolbus_en.html

Klaude's musical instrument is from Germany. You can make your own musical instruments:
http://www.dsokids.com/activities-at-home/
   make-instrument/.aspx

About the Author

J. L. Anderson solves a mystery of her own almost every day like figuring out why her daughter is suddenly so quiet (what did she get into this time?), which of her two dogs stole the bag of treats, where her husband is taking her for a surprise dinner, or what happened to her keys this time. You can learn more about J.L. Anderson at www.jessicaleeanderson.com.

About the Illustrator

I have always loved drawing from a very young age. While I was at school, most of my time was spent drawing comics and copying my favorite characters. With a portfolio under my arm, I started drawing comics for newspapers and fanzines. After I finished my studies I decided to try to make a living as a freelance illustrator... and here I am!